THE WIND IN THE WILLOWS

The Open Road

Re-told by Anne McKie. Illustrated by Ken McKie.

"Ratty," said Mole suddenly one bright summer morning, "if you please, I want to ask you a favour. Will you take me to meet Mr. Toad?"

"Why, certainly," said the good natured Rat jumping to his feet. "Get the boat out and we'll paddle up there at once. It's never the wrong time to call on Toad. Early or late he's always the same fellow. Always good tempered, always glad to see you, always sorry when you go."

"He must be a very nice animal," said the Mole, as he got into the boat and took the oars.

"He is the very best of animals," the Rat went on. "So simple, so good natured, and so affectionate. Perhaps he is a bit boastful - but he has got some great qualities has Toady!"

Rounding a bend in the river, they saw a handsome old house built of mellow red brick, with lawns reaching down to the water's edge.

"There's Toad Hall," said the Rat. "Toad is very rich, and this is one of the nicest houses in these parts, though we never admit as much to Toad!"

As they glided up the creek, they passed a large boathouse. It was full of beautiful boats, but not one in the water. The place looked quite forgotten.

The Rat looked around him. "I understand that Toad is fed up with boats now! I wonder what his new craze is? No doubt we shall find out soon enough!"

Mole and Ratty stepped out of their boat and strolled across the lawns in search of Toad. They found him sitting in a wicker garden chair, a large map spread out in front of him.

"Hooray!" he cried jumping up. "This is splendid!" He shook the paws of both animals warmly (he never even asked to be introduced to Mole).

"How kind of you!" he went on, dancing round them. "I was just going to send a boat down the river for you, Ratty, with strict orders for you to be fetched up here at once. Come inside both of you!"

"Let's sit quiet a bit, Toady!" said the Rat, throwing himself into an armchair, while Mole took another by the side of him. "Were you going to ask my advice about rowing?" asked the Rat.

"Oh, pooh! boating!" interrupted Toad in disgust. "What a waste of time - gave that up long ago. No, I've discovered an interest to last me a lifetime!"

A very excited Mr. Toad led the way to the stable yard; and there, drawn out of the coach house and into the open, they saw a gipsy caravan shining and new, painted a canary-yellow picked out with green, and red wheels.

"There you are!" cried Toad, standing before them legs apart, chest out. "There's real life for you. The open road, the dusty highway, villages, towns, cities. Here today and somewhere else tomorrow. Come inside and look. Planned it all myself, I did!"

The Mole was very interested and excited, and followed Toad up the steps and into the caravan. Rat only snorted and thrust his hands deep into his pockets, remaining where he was.

It was indeed very compact and comfortable. Little sleeping bunks - a little table that folded up against the wall - a cooking stove, lockers, bookshelves, a bird cage with a bird in it, and pots, pans, jugs and kettles of every shape and size.

"All complete!" said Toad triumphantly, pulling open a locker. "You see - biscuits, potted lobster, sardines - everything you could possibly want. Soda water here - tobacco there - notepaper, bacon, jam, cards and dominoes. You'll find that nothing whatever has been forgotten, when we make our start this afternoon!"

"I beg your pardon," said Rat slowly. "Did I overhear you say that we make a start this afternoon?"

"Now, you dear, good old Ratty," pleaded Toad, "you must come, I can't possibly manage without you. You can't possibly want to stay on your smelly old river all your life. I want to show you the world!"

"I don't care," said the Rat stubbornly. "I'm not coming, and that's that. I'm going to stay on my smelly old river. And what's more, Mole is too, aren't you, Mole?"

"Of course I am," said Mole loyally. "I'll always stick to you, Ratty. All the same, it sounds as if it might have been fun!"

The Rat could see that his friend Mole would really love to go and he hated to disappoint him.

During lunch, Toad painted such a wonderful picture of life in a caravan, that Mole could hardly sit in his chair for excitement.

Somehow, it soon seemed taken for granted by all three of them that the trip was settled.

Ratty couldn't bear to disappoint his two dear friends and that was the only reason he agreed to go.

When they were quite ready, Toad led Ratty and Mole to the paddock to try to capture the old grey horse who was going to pull the caravan. However, the horse preferred to stay in his paddock - and took a great deal of catching.

At last the horse was harnessed and they set off, all talking at once!

It was a lovely afternoon. They walked along either side of the cart or sat on the shaft, kicking up the dust as they went.

From the orchards by the road, birds whistled to them cheerily. People passing them called "Good day," or stopped to say nice things about their beautiful caravan; and the rabbits, sitting at their front doors in the hedgerows, held up their paws and said, "Oh my! Oh my! Oh my!"

Late in the evening, tired and happy and miles from home, they drew up on a common, far away from any houses or people.

They turned the horse loose to graze, and ate their simple supper sitting on the grass by the side of the caravan. Toad boasted about all he was going to do in the days to come, while the stars came out and a yellow moon appeared as if from nowhere.

At last they turned into their little bunks in the caravan; and Toad, kicking out his legs, sleepily said, "Well, good night, you fellows! This is the real life for a gentleman! Talk about your old river!"

"I don't talk about my river," replied the Rat patiently. "You know I don't, Toad. But I think about it," he added sadly. "I think about it - all the time."

The Mole reached out from under his blanket, felt for the Rat's paw in the darkness and gave it a squeeze. "I'll do whatever you like, Ratty," he whispered. "Shall we run away tomorrow morning, quite early - very early - and go back to our dear old hole on the river?"

"No, no, we'll see it out," whispered back the Rat. "Thanks awfully, but I ought to stick by Toad till this trip is ended. It wouldn't be safe for him to be left to himself. It won't take very long. His fads never do. Good night!"

The end was indeed nearer than even the Rat suspected.

After so much open air and excitement the Toad slept very soundly, and no amount of shaking could get him out of bed next morning. So the Mole and the Rat set to work.

The Rat saw to the horse, and lit a fire, cleaned last night's cups and plates, then got things ready for breakfast.

The Mole trudged off to the nearest village, a long way off, for milk and eggs and everything that Toad had forgotten to provide.

The hard work had all been done, and the two animals were resting, quite tired out, by the time Toad appeared on the scene. He was fresh and bright, remarking about a pleasant easy life they were all leading now, after all the cares and worries of house-keeping at home.

They had a pleasant ramble that day over grassy downs and along narrow lanes. They camped that night, as before, on a grassy common. Only this time Rat and Mole took care that Toad should do his fair share of the work.

Now when the time came for starting next morning, Toad was not so happy about his new easy life. In fact, he tried to get back into his bunk, until Ratty and Mole pulled him out by force.

They went on their way, as before, across country by narrow lanes, and it was not till the afternoon that they came out on to the highway. It was their first highway. It was there that disaster, sudden and unexpected, struck them.

So great was the disaster - that Toad would never be the same again!

They were strolling along the road quite slowly. Mole was by the horse's head, chatting to him (as the poor thing had been feeling a bit left out). Toad and Rat were walking behind the cart talking together. At least Toad was talking and Rat was listening!

When, suddenly from behind them, they heard a faint warning hum, like the drone of a distant bee. Glancing back, they saw a small cloud of dust with a dark centre coming towards them at incredible speed, while from out of the dust a faint "Poop-poop!" could be heard.

Toad and Mole went on talking when, all of a sudden, a blast of wind and a whirl of sound made them jump for the nearest ditch.

The "Poop-poop" rang with a blaring shout in their ears. They had a moment's glimpse of the inside of a magnificent glittering motor car, with its driver hugging tight onto its wheel.

It flung a cloud of dust that blinded and totally covered Toad, Rat and Mole. Then it disappeared to a speck in the distance, sounding like a droning bee once more.

The old grey horse, dreaming, as he plodded along, of his quiet paddock, had never had such a fright! Rearing, plunging, backing steadily (in spite of Mole's efforts to calm him) he drove the cart backwards towards the deep ditch at the side of the road. It wavered an instant - then there was a heart-rending crash - and the canary-coloured cart lay on its side in the ditch, a total wreck!

The Rat danced up and down the road in temper. "You villains!" he shouted, shaking both fists. "You scoundrels, you road-hogs! I'll have the law on you!" His homesickness all forgotten.

Toad sat in the middle of the dusty road, his legs stretched out in front of him, simply staring at the disappearing motor car, with a very strange expression on his face, quietly murmuring, "Poop-poop!"

The Mole was busy trying to quieten the horse, which he managed to do after a time.

Then he went to look at the caravan on its side in the ditch. It was a sorry sight! Panels and windows smashed, axles hopelessly bent, sardine tins scattered all over the wide world and the poor bird in the cage calling to be let out.

The Rat came over to help Mole, but both of them were not strong enough to right the caravan. "Hi! Toad!" they cried. "Come and lend a hand, can't you!"

The Toad never answered a word, or budged from his seat in the road, so they went to see what was the matter with him.

They found him in a sort of dream, a happy smile on his face, his eyes fixed on the cloud of dust left by the speeding motor car. Every so often Rat and Mole heard him murmur, "Poop-poop!"

The Rat shook him by the shoulder. "Are you coming to help us, Toad?" he demanded sternly.

"Glorious, stirring sight!" murmured Toad, never offering to move. "The real way to travel. The only way to travel. Here today - in next week tomorrow. Oh bliss! Oh poop-poop! Oh my! Oh my!"

"Oh stop being a fool, Toad!" cried the Mole in despair.

"And to think I never knew," the Toad went on, "all those wasted years that lie behind me. But now that I know, now that I fully realise. What dust clouds shall spring up behind me as I speed along! What carts shall I fling carelessly into the ditch. Horrid little carts - common carts - canary-coloured carts!"

"What are we to do with him?" asked the Mole of the Water Rat.

"Nothing at all," replied the Rat firmly. "You see I know him of old. He's got a new craze, and it always takes him this way. He'll be like this for days now. Never mind him. Let's go and see what can be done about the caravan."

They inspected the caravan most carefully, it was damaged beyond repair. The axles were in a hopeless state, and the missing wheel was shattered into pieces.

The Rat knotted the horse's reins over his back and took him by the lead, carrying the birdcage in the other hand. "Come on!" he said grimly to Mole. "It's five or six miles to the nearest town, and we shall have to walk it. The sooner we make a start the better!"

"But what about Toad?" asked the Mole anxiously, as they set off together. "We can't leave him here, sitting in the middle of the road by himself, the state he is in. It's not safe. Suppose another motor car were to come along."

"Oh bother Toad," said the Rat angrily, "I've done with him."

They had not gone very far on their way, when there was a pattering of feet behind them, and Toad caught them up and thrust a paw inside the elbow of each of them; still panting and staring into space.

"Now look here, Toad," said the Rat sharply, "as soon as we get to town, you'll have to go straight to the police station. See who owns that motor car and make a complaint about it. And then you'll have to find a blacksmith to mend the caravan. Meanwhile the Mole and I will go to an inn and find comfortable rooms where we can stay until the caravan's ready and till your nerves have got over the shock!"

"Police station!" murmured Toad dreamily. "Me complain about that beautiful, that heavenly motor car. Never!

"As for mending that cart! I've done with carts for ever. I never want to see or hear of it again. Oh, Ratty. Thank you for coming with me on this trip. Without you I might never have seen that wonderful motor car. I owe it all to you, my best of friends!"

The Rat turned from him in despair. "He's quite hopeless. I give up!" he said to Mole. "When we get to town we'll go to the railway station and catch a train that will take us back to the River Bank tonight!"

After a very long tiring walk they finally reached the town. They went straight to the railway station and left Toad in the waiting room, giving a porter two pence to keep a strict eye on him.

Then they left the horse at an inn stable, and left word for the caravan to be mended and returned to Toad.

Eventually, a slow train took them to a station not very far from Toad Hall.

The Rat and the Mole helped the spellbound, sleep-walking Toad to his door, put him inside, and asked his housekeeper to feed him and see he got to bed.

Then they got their boat from the boathouse, rowed down the river, and at a very late hour sat down to supper in their own snug little riverside parlour, to the Rat's great joy and contentment.

The following evening the Mole, who had got up late and taken things very easy all day, was sitting on the bank fishing, when the Rat, who had been looking up his friends and gossiping, came strolling along to find him.

"Heard the news?" he said. "There's nothing else being talked about, all along the river bank. Toad went up to town by an early train this morning. And he has ordered a large and very expensive motor car."

But that will be another story...

This book belongs to

_____

_____

_____

Age _____

Published by Grandreams Books Ltd,
4 North Parade, Bath, BA1 1LF, UK.

Grandreams Books Inc.,
360 Hurst Street, Linden, NJ 07036 USA
Printed in China.

Favourite Tales in this book

SINBAD

Once upon a time, in the faraway city of
Bagdad, there lived a young man whose name was
Sinbad. He longed for adventure, and that is why he
sailed the seven seas.

One day, Sinbad sailed away on one of many
journeys. After many days at sea, his ship dropped
anchor at a tiny island, and Sinbad and the other
sailors stepped ashore to look around.

All at once, the island seemed to grow and
rise up out of the water. It was no island, but a
monster whale! Suddenly, the whale took a great dive
beneath the waves, and everyone fell off into the sea.

All the other sailors managed to swim back to
the ship, but poor Sinbad was left behind floating in
the water, clinging to a piece of driftwood.

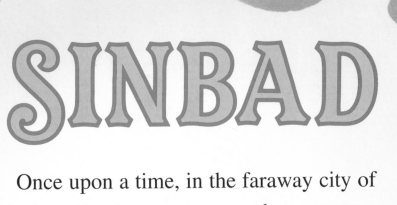

After a while he was washed ashore on another island. He ran across the sandy beach and climbed the tallest palm tree, to try to see his ship. But alas, Sinbad had been left all alone, and his ship was nowhere to be seen.

As he gazed down from the tree, Sinbad noticed a huge white egg on the sand. He slid down the trunk to take a better look. All of a sudden, a big black shadow passed over him. There, circling overhead, was a great white bird – almost as big as the island.

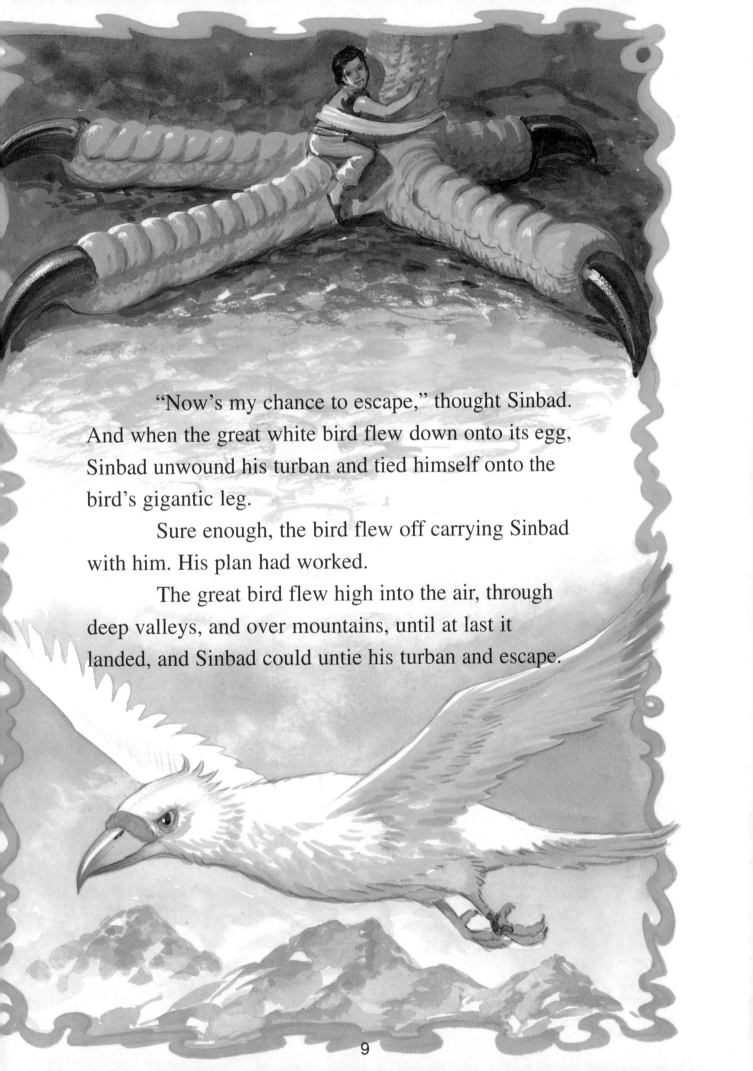

"Now's my chance to escape," thought Sinbad. And when the great white bird flew down onto its egg, Sinbad unwound his turban and tied himself onto the bird's gigantic leg.

Sure enough, the bird flew off carrying Sinbad with him. His plan had worked.

The great bird flew high into the air, through deep valleys, and over mountains, until at last it landed, and Sinbad could untie his turban and escape.

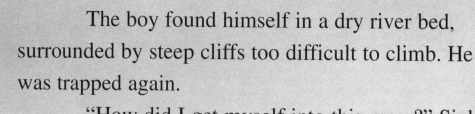

The boy found himself in a dry river bed, surrounded by steep cliffs too difficult to climb. He was trapped again.

"How did I get myself into this mess?" Sinbad cried out loudly, his voice echoing around the cliffs.

All of a sudden, there came a loud hissing noise. All around poor Sinbad large serpents slithered across the floor. Underneath the snakes were huge diamonds and gems – some as big as Sinbad himself.

At the sight of so much treasure, Sinbad's eyes opened wide. Then he remembered the snakes and ran to the nearest cave for safety.

"I can hear voices," cried Sinbad in delight. "Someone is here to rescue me." The boy looked up and saw faces peering over the edge of the cliffs. Men were throwing something onto the rocks below. Could it be huge pieces of meat?

At once, Sinbad understood what was happening. These men threw lumps of meat onto the diamonds near the snakes, then the mountain eagles would swoop down, grab the meat, and carry it back to their nests. Sometimes a few of the diamonds would stick to the meat, and then the men would grab the gems from the eagles' nests.

Sinbad waited for the biggest bird to swoop down. He grabbed the largest diamond he could find and clung onto the bird's legs with all his might.

And that is how our adventurer, Sinbad, escaped the snakes. And that is how he came to be sitting in an eagle's nest with the biggest diamond of them all.

Sinbad returned home a rich man. After a while he got tired of doing nothing and made up his mind to set sail on another voyage.

After many days at sea, his ship dropped anchor in the harbour of a large city.

When the people saw Sinbad and his crew, they begged him for help. "Our markets are quite empty of fruit. We have nothing to sell and nothing to buy," they moaned. "We have no coconuts or dates, no pomegranates or figs, not even one banana."

Sinbad looked puzzled, until the people explained, "Our trees are so tall and smooth, it is impossible for anyone to climb them, except the monkeys."

"Leave it to us," laughed Sinbad and his sailors. And they set off to find the trees in the forest.

When the ship's crew saw the monkeys who lived in the top branches, it gave them an idea. The sailors looked around for stones, which they threw at the monkeys, who thought it was some sort of game. The mischievous monkeys pelted the sailors with coconuts and fruit, who, in turn, filled up great sacks with them.

They returned to the city and gave the food to the hungry people. Everyone was very grateful and Sinbad and his crew sailed away with many presents and thanks from the city.

No sooner had Sinbad gone back home to Bagdad, than the Caliph sent for him. "Set sail at once," he commanded, "and take these gifts to my friend the Sultan of Tasmir Island."

So once more, Sinbad and his crew put to sea, but alas, on the way, the ship was attacked by pirates, who captured all on board. At the very next port these cruel pirates sold Sinbad and his crew as slaves.

Sinbad was bought by a wealthy merchant who had a lovely daughter. "Slave," grinned the merchant, "I have a very dangerous task for you," and he dragged Sinbad deep into the forest.

"In a few moments the biggest elephant in the world will pass this way to drink at the river. Take this bow and arrow and shoot him," and at that, the merchant pushed Sinbad up a tree and ran away.

All at once, Sinbad could feel the trees shaking. Thundering down the path came an enormous elephant with gleaming tusks. Sinbad shook with fright!

The poor boy trembled so much that he lost his balance and fell out of the tree. He landed on top of the elephant and slid down his trunk onto the ground. Sinbad closed his eyes tight, for he was certain the elephant's great foot would crush him to a pulp.

A soft voice was speaking to the great elephant, it was the merchant's daughter. She was standing in the middle of the forest patch – feeding him bread and fruit from a silver dish.

Sinbad could hardly believe his eyes. "Don't be afraid," said the girl. "I come here every night to feed this beautiful creature. My father is a cruel man. He wants to kill my elephant and cut off his tusks to sell for ivory."

When the girl put her arms around the beast's great trunk, Sinbad could see how gentle the elephant was.

"Come," smiled Sinbad, "let us escape from here." Quickly he helped the girl onto the elephant. "We will ride away this very night on the elephant's back, and he will carry us back home to Bagdad."

So off they went together travelling over many miles and many lands, until they arrived back safely… and lived happily ever after.

THE THREE LITTLE PIGS

Once upon a time, there was a Mother Pig who lived on a farm with her three little piglets, in a warm and comfortable sty.

They were very happy together and got on very well with all the other animals. The farmer gave them plenty to eat. He filled up their trough twice a day with as many turnips and juicy apples as they could manage.

As you may know, pigs are very fond of their food, so it came as no surprise when the little pigs grew too large for the farmyard.

Mother Pig gazed at them with pride, "You have grown so big now, that you must go out into the world and build new houses for yourselves."

As they waved goodbye, their mother gave them some good advice. "Always remember," she said with a tear in her eye, "to beware of the Big Bad Wolf." So, off the three little pigs went, singing and whistling down the road.

Before very long, they came to a stack of straw. "It must be my lucky day," chuckled the first little pig. "I shall build my house with straw, right on this very spot!" Quickly, he gathered up the straw – and in next to no time he had built himself a little house.

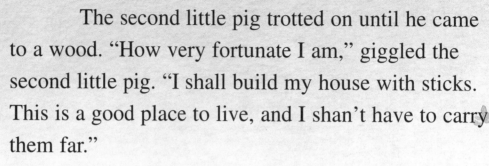

The second little pig trotted on until he came to a wood. "How very fortunate I am," giggled the second little pig. "I shall build my house with sticks. This is a good place to live, and I shan't have to carry them far."

So, he set to work and soon had a fine wooden house, with windows and doors and even a wooden chimney. The second little pig felt quite safe from the Big Bad Wolf, so he settled down to eat his dinner.

Now, the third little pig was much wiser than the other two. He planned to build his house of bricks – and had brought along the tools to do the job. He worked very hard for a long time before his house was finished and he was safe inside.

All this time, the Big Bad Wolf had been keeping his eye on the three little pigs.

Sure enough, one dreadful day, the Big Bad Wolf came knocking on the first little pig's door and said, "Little pig, little pig, can I come in?"

"Not by the hair on my chinny, chin chin, you cannot come in," squealed the first little pig.

"Then I'll huff and I'll puff and I'll blow your house down," said the wolf. So he huffed and he puffed, and in no time at all the straw house had blown away – and the wolf gobbled up the first little pig.

Next day, the wolf went to see where the second little pig lived. It didn't take him long to find the house made of sticks. When the second little pig heard the wolf coming, he hurried inside and locked the door.

The Big Bad Wolf banged on the door and cried, "Little pig, little pig, can I come in?"

"Not by the hair on my chinny, chin chin, you cannot come in," squealed the second little pig.

"Then I'll huff and I'll puff and I'll blow your house down," said the wolf. So he huffed and he puffed, and in no time at all the stick house just fell to pieces – and the wolf gobbled up the second little pig.

It wasn't very long before the wolf found the brick house built by the third little pig. He marched up the path and banged on the door, "Little pig, little pig, can I come in?"

"Not by the hair on my chinny, chin chin, you cannot come in," squealed the third little pig.

"Then I'll huff and I'll puff and I'll blow your house down," said the wolf. So he huffed and he puffed – but the brick house did not fall down.

The furious wolf ran at the house and banged and kicked the walls, trying to knock them down. But still the brick house did not fall in. So the wolf had to give up and go home.

"I haven't seen the last of him," the little pig thought to himself. And, of course, he was right.

That crafty wolf made his mind up to trick the last little pig and make a tasty meal of him. So the very next day the wolf shouted through the little pig's window, "Come with me tomorrow morning at six o'clock and we will dig some turnips for ourselves from the farmer's field."

But, the clever little pig got up an hour early, and when the wolf called for him, he was back safe inside his brick house, eating the turnips.

Then, the wolf said, "Meet me at five tomorrow morning and we can pick apples together from that tree over there."

At four the next morning, the little pig climbed
the tree to pick apples. But just as he reached the top,
he saw the wolf waiting underneath – ready to eat him.

"These apples are so juicy," called the little
pig, throwing one far from the tree. And while the wolf
ran for the apple, the clever little pig jumped down and
ran all the way home.

Still that Big Bad Wolf wouldn't give up.
"Come with me to the fair at four this afternoon," he
begged the little pig.

So at two o'clock the
third little pig trotted off to the
fair to ride on the roundabouts
and swings. As he had some
money left, he bought himself a
butterchurn.

On his way home, as he reached the top of the
hill, he spied the wolf coming towards him. So he
jumped inside the butterchurn.

It toppled over and began to roll down the hill.
Faster and faster it went, until it rolled right over the
wolf and knocked him flat. The little pig ran home,
shaken, but safe and sound.

Later that night the little pig heard a noise on his roof! It was the Big Bad Wolf!

"I am going to climb down your chimney and eat you up," the wolf shouted, as he began to climb down.

Quick as he could, the little pig took the lid of a huge pot boiling on his fire. The Big Bad Wolf came sliding down the chimney and fell with a splash straight into the boiling pot.

And that, I'm happy to say, was the end of him.

But it wasn't the end of the third little pig. He was far too clever for that Big Bad Wolf.

THE UGLY DUCKLING

It was summertime. The sky was blue and the air was filled with the scent of meadow flowers – and the sound of bees buzzing from flower to flower made Mother Duck feel very sleepy.

She had been sitting on her nest all summer long, hidden deep in the reeds on the edge of a pond. The Mother Duck felt rather lonely all by herself, "I do wish my ducklings would hatch," she sighed, "then I would have someone to talk to and join me in a dip in the pond."

29

At long last the eggs began to crack open. First one, then another and another, until all the ducklings had popped out of their shells. Their soft yellow down soon dried out in the warm summer sun. In next to no time they were all eager to discover their new world.

The baby ducklings jumped out of their nest and ran into the reeds. Some of them hid, and of course, some of them got lost. "Peep, peep! What a big world," they all cried darting everywhere. Poor Mother Duck felt quite muddled.

"A bit of peace and quiet is what I need," she quacked as she waddled back to her nest to rest. It was then she noticed one egg that had not hatched. "How strange," she thought. "This egg is so big, it doesn't look like mine at all."

But she sat down all the same, just to keep it warm. At last the big egg cracked. Out tumbled a duckling twice as big as the rest. Sad to say compared to the others, he could only be described as ugly.

Poor Mother Duck shook her feathers as she gazed at her huge duckling, "How big and ugly you are. Not a bit like the others."

It was time to take her new family down to the pond for a swim. One by one the ducklings jumped into the water with a splash. Then up they bobbed, swimming along beautifully – especially the Ugly Duckling.

How quickly they could swim across the pond, following their mother in a straight line. "What a wonderful place the world is," cheeped the ducklings. Then one by one they hopped out of the pond and into the farmyard.

What a noisy place it was. Full of ducks and hens pushing and pecking at each other, and fighting over every scrap of food in the place.

Sad to say, nobody liked the Ugly Duckling. Perhaps it was because he was different, and not soft and fluffy like all the other baby birds.

"He's so ugly," clucked one old hen. "I've never seen anything so awkward in all my days." And she tried to peck the Ugly Duckling's legs.

This made the poor duckling feel terribly unhappy. "I am so ugly, I will go far away so no-one can look at me."

So he ran through the fields until he came to the marshes where the wild ducks lived. But he found no welcome there! They hissed at him and stabbed at him with their black beaks until he ran away again.

As darkness fell the Ugly Duckling came to an old cottage. He crept under the door and stayed all night in the warmth. Next morning an old woman with a cat and a hen found him. "Can you lay duck eggs?" she asked. The Ugly Duckling shook his head.

"Then you'll have to go," snarled the cat as she chased him out the door.

And so the Ugly Duckling made up his mind to find a place to hide where no-one would see how ugly he was. For weeks and weeks he lived alone by a lake. Summer had gone and winter was on its way.

One evening a flock of lovely white birds flew overhead. The duckling gazed up at them in wonder. "If only I could be as beautiful as that!" and he began to cry.

That night was so cold that the lake turned to ice. The Ugly Duckling was so tired he fell asleep and froze fast to the ice.

Very early next day, luckily for the
Ugly Duckling, a passing farmer found him. He
cracked the ice with his stick and freed the duckling.
He pushed him inside his warm jacket and carried
him home to his wife.

"I could fatten him up,"
she said. "In a few weeks he'll
make a fine roast dinner."

Unfortunately, the farmer's
two children were very naughty.
All day long they chased the
duckling round the kitchen trying
to grab him.

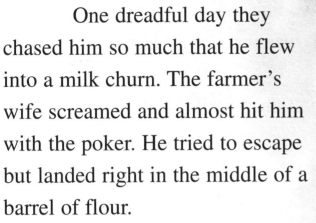

One dreadful day they chased him so much that he flew into a milk churn. The farmer's wife screamed and almost hit him with the poker. He tried to escape but landed right in the middle of a barrel of flour.

In the upset that followed, the Ugly Duckling darted out of the kitchen door, and never stopped until he reached a peaceful lake.

There he stayed, sad and lonely all winter long, until spring came.

Somehow the warm sun made the duckling feel glad to be alive. As he swam out of his hiding place in the reeds, three snow white swans glided towards him.

The Ugly Duckling bowed his head, waiting for them to peck and hiss at him. It was then he saw his reflection in the water.

No longer was he a big clumsy Ugly Duckling – but a graceful white swan.

"Fly away with us," said the swans. So, happy at last, the new swan spread his wings and flew away with them across the lake.

PETER PAN

Here is the story of Peter Pan – the boy who never wants to grow up. He comes from Never Never Land, an island which children sometimes visit in their dreams. The most magical thing about Peter Pan is… he can fly!

This favourite of all stories begins in a large house in London. It's the home of Mr. and Mrs. Darling, parents of Wendy, Michael and John. Now, these three children have a very unusual nurse, a great big Newfoundland dog called Nana!

Why, you might ask, did Peter Pan ever visit the home of the Darlings? Sometimes, when he was feeling lonely, he would fly up to their nursery window and peep inside – just to be part of a human family again and remember what it was like to have a mother.

If the nursery window was left open and Nana the dog was nowhere about, Peter would fly right into the nursery. Wendy often caught a glimpse of the strange boy – but she thought she was just dreaming.

Now one night, Mrs. Darling was sitting sewing while her children slept. Peter flew straight in through the window. He didn't notice that Nana was in the nursery. The dog sprang up and growled and snarled at the boy. As he tried to escape, his shadow caught on the window – and Peter had to leave it behind. Rather startled, Mrs. Darling picked it up and put it in a drawer.

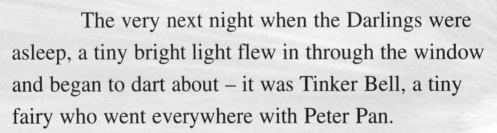

The very next night when the Darlings were asleep, a tiny bright light flew in through the window and began to dart about – it was Tinker Bell, a tiny fairy who went everywhere with Peter Pan.

She was searching for Peter's shadow. She looked in all the cupboards, all the drawers, she even delved inside a jug. Eventually she found the right place just as Peter flew in through the window.

He grabbed his shadow and shut the drawer tight, trapping poor Tinker Bell inside. He searched around trying to find something that would stick his shadow back on.

All this noise woke up Wendy. She knew what to do straight away. She fetched her workbox, and very neatly stitched the shadow on again.

When Wendy offered Peter a kiss he looked puzzled. He had never had a kiss before and held his hand out for a present. So Wendy gave him her silver thimble instead. In return, Peter gave her one of his acorn-shaped buttons, which Wendy hung on a chain round her neck.

As Peter sat in the nursery he told Wendy all about Never Never Land where he lived with the Lost Boys and the fairies. He explained to her how a fairy dies every time a human child says, "I do not believe in fairies!"

It was then that Peter remembered Tinker Bell still trapped in the drawer. He let her out, and she was furious. She buzzed round Wendy and tried to pull her hair. Perhaps she was jealous of Peter's new friend!

All this noise woke up John and Michael. They listened spellbound when Peter told them about his fierce fights with the pirates on Never Never Land. And, of course, they wanted to go.

So it was agreed that they should first learn to fly, and go away with Peter Pan that very night.

After a great deal of practise they were ready. Not a moment too soon, for running up the stairs came Mr. and Mrs. Darling.

One by one the children flew out of the nursery window, leaving their poor parents behind. Soon they were soaring through the night sky with the lights of London far below them.

On and on they went. "Second star to the right and on until morning," cried Peter Pan as he sped ahead.

At long last, as the sun rose, they glimpsed Never Never Land beneath them. It was just as Peter had said. Anchored near the island was the pirate ship, the Jolly Roger, with its evil Captain Hook. The pirate chief hated Pan because he had cut off his hand and thrown it to a crocodile, who longed to eat the rest of him. Luckily the crocodile had swallowed a clock, and everyone could hear him coming with his loud 'tick, tick, tick'.

As they flew over the island, Wendy and the boys saw an Indian tribe round their wigwams. These were the Indians who were always on the trail of the evil pirates.

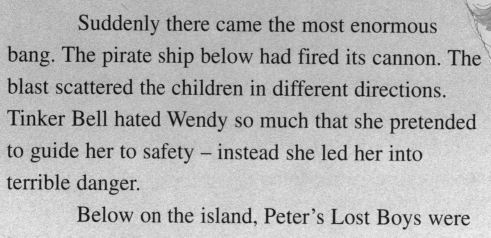

Suddenly there came the most enormous bang. The pirate ship below had fired its cannon. The blast scattered the children in different directions. Tinker Bell hated Wendy so much that she pretended to guide her to safety – instead she led her into terrible danger.

Below on the island, Peter's Lost Boys were looking up into the sky. They saw Wendy and thought she was a bird. "Peter wants you to shoot Wendy," cried Tinker Bell.

So the biggest boy took his bow and arrow and shot Wendy through the heart. She fluttered down from the sky and landed on the ground. Luckily the arrow had struck into the acorn-shaped button Peter had given her, and she was quite unharmed.

Peter was so angry, he banished the wicked Tinker Bell for a whole week, which made her hate Wendy even more.

Eagerly the Lost Boys led Wendy to their secret home underground. To reach it, they squeezed through holes in certain tree trunks, then slid down into a huge cave below.

Wendy, John and Michael lived with the Lost Boys for weeks. Wendy did their washing, cooked all their meals, and told them stories like a real mother. She told such lovely stories about her home and her mother that John and Michael wanted to go back home. The Lost Boys begged to be allowed to go there too.

This hurt Peter's feelings. He was afraid to leave Never Never Land for good, in case he grew up. However, he told Tinker Bell to guide them back home over the sea. Then sadly he shook hands with Wendy.

"Promise you will drink your glass of medicine every night when I am gone." The words were hardly out of her mouth, when the air was filled with a bloodcurdling scream.

45

The pirates were attacking the Indians in the forest above the Lost Boys' home. It was a bitter battle, and sad to say, the pirates won. The Lost Boys, however, thought their friends the Indians had won. So one by one they climbed out of their secret cave.

The evil pirates were waiting; they pounced on them and captured them all. They tied everyone up and took them aboard the Jolly Roger.

But Captain Hook stayed behind. He was out to kill Peter Pan! He peered down all the hollow trees until he spied Peter asleep in the secret cave below. He squeezed his arm down the tree trunk and slipped five drops of deadly poison into Peter's medicine glass that Wendy had left.

Later that night, Peter was woken up by Tinker Bell, who told him of Wendy's capture. Quickly, Peter jumped out of bed to take his medicine as he had promised. Tinker Bell knew it was deadly poison – as she had heard Captain Hook talking about it in the forest.

Bravely she flew up to the glass and drank the medicine herself. As she fell to the floor, her tiny fairy light was almost gone. She was going to die.

Peter stood up and shouted in his loudest voice, "If you believe in fairies, clap your hands." It seemed as if all the air was full of noise – made by all the children in the world. Tinker Bell was saved!

The evil Captain Hook had tied Wendy to the mast and was about to make the Lost Boys walk the plank. All at once he stopped. He fell on the deck in fear. 'Tick, tick, tick'. He thought it was the crocodile.

In fact it was Peter Pan imitating it. While Hook was hiding in fear, Peter slipped on board and freed everybody.

48

Then began the terrible fight with Hook. They clashed swords up and down the deck of the ship, until at last, Hook overbalanced and fell into the sea – where his friend the crocodile was waiting.

What joy it was for Wendy, John and Michael to return home. How happy the Darlings were to see their children home safely.

It is said that the Darlings adopted all the Lost Boys, and that Wendy goes back to Never Never Land every year to see Peter Pan – perhaps you may go there one day too!

JACK AND THE BEANSTALK

This is the story of a young boy named Jack, who lived in a tumbledown cottage with his mother.

They were so poor they had barely enough money for food. One day, Jack's mother found to her despair that they had no money left at all – not even one penny.

"There is only one thing left to do," sighed Jack's mother, "we must sell our cow Buttercup, as she is the only thing we have left in the world."

So Jack promised to go to market the following day to sell Buttercup for as much money as he could.

Early next morning before it was light, Jack left for market. He crept out of the house while his mother was still asleep. She was very fond of the cow, and would have found it hard to say goodbye.

Jack hadn't gone very far along the road before he met a pedlar.

"I will buy your cow in exchange for these five magic beans," the stranger said as he held out his hand. "Plant them and you will grow rich."

Young Jack couldn't resist. He gave Buttercup to the pedlar, grabbed the magic beans, and ran home to tell his mother.

She was rather surprised to see him back from the market so soon. When she heard about the magic beans, she was so angry she tossed them out of the window. And poor silly Jack was sent to bed without any supper.

The next morning dawned dark and gloomy. Jack jumped out of bed and looked out of the window. The sky above was dark – not with clouds – but with giant green leaves! To Jack's amazement the magic beans had grown in the night. They were so tall, they covered the tiny cottage and disappeared up into the sky.

Jack had to push open the cottage door with all his might. He stepped outside and began to climb the beanstalk. The branches of the bean plant were so thick they formed a ladder, and soon Jack had climbed so high that his cottage was just a tiny speck down below.

At last the branches grew thinner and Jack knew he had reached the top. Ahead of him was a long road, which led to a mysterious castle in the distance. Bravely, Jack marched along until he reached the castle door. Loudly he knocked and waited.

It was opened by the most enormous woman Jack had ever seen. "Come in and eat," her great voice boomed. "Beware my husband the Giant – or he will eat you!"

Jack turned pale. "Don't be afraid," laughed the Giantess as she led Jack into her kitchen. The kind woman gave him a plate of food almost as high as himself. Jack had only taken two mouthfuls, when the whole room began to shake.

"My husband the Giant is home," cried the Giantess, and with that, she pushed Jack into the cupboard.

Not a moment too soon, for when the Giant strode into the room, he began to sniff around Jack's cupboard:

"Fee, fi, fo, fum,
I smell the blood of an Englishman;
Be he alive or be he dead,
I'll grind his bones to make my bread."

His wife smiled, "It's only the giant meat pie I cooked for your dinner that you can smell."

When he had gobbled up every scrap of food,
the Giant hammered on the table with his great fists.
"Wife," he called, "bring me my hen that lays golden eggs."

Jack could hardly believe his eyes when he
peeped out of the cupboard.

"Lay golden eggs," commanded the Giant.
And the little brown hen, which the Giant had placed
on the table, began to lay golden eggs. The Giant
scooped up the eggs, put them in his pocket and fell
fast asleep.

Jack saw his chance. He
jumped out of the cupboard,
snatched up the hen and ran for
his life until he reached the top
of the beanstalk.

He slid down the thick branches at top speed. His mother was overjoyed to see him back safe and sound. The little brown hen laid lots of eggs and made their fortune. Jack bought back their cow, Buttercup, and all three of them were very happy.

After a while, Jack longed to climb the beanstalk once more. So early one morning, before anyone could stop him, he climbed it again in search of adventure. Higher and higher he went, until he saw the winding road he knew led to the Giant's castle. Once again the castle door was opened by the Giant's wife. She didn't recognise Jack because of his fine new clothes, so she asked him in.

No sooner had Jack reached the kitchen, than the Giant returned. Jack looked around in panic.

"Hide in the log basket by the oven," begged the Giant's frightened wife.

Sure enough, the Giant strode straight over to where Jack was hiding.

"Fee, fi, fo, fum,

I smell the blood of an Englishman;

Be he alive or be he dead,

I'll grind his bones to make my bread."

"It's only the soup I made for you this morning," said his wife, as she placed the huge bowl on the table in front of him.

What a noise the Giant made drinking his soup! As soon as he had finished, he took down a beautiful golden harp from the shelf above him. "Play me a lullaby," the Giant commanded the golden harp.

Jack had never heard such lovely music in his life. He knew he must have the harp for his very own. Such sweet music came from the harp, that the Giant soon fell into a deep sleep.

Jack saw his chance and seized the harp from the table. But as he ran out of the castle gates, the harp began to play loudly, "Help me, Master. Help me!"

The Giant awoke just in time to see Jack disappearing with his harp out of the castle gates. He thundered after the boy, screaming and roaring: "You stole my hen – you shall not have my golden harp!" And he chased Jack towards the beanstalk.

59

Jack slid down the branches in fear of his life. He could feel the beanstalk swaying and cracking as the Giant began to climb down after him. Now the Giant was as slow as Jack was nimble. So, when the boy reached the bottom of the beanstalk, he grabbed an axe and chopped at the branches with all his might.

The whole thing began to sway. With a few more blows of Jack's axe, the whole beanstalk came crashing down – bringing the Giant with it. His great weight made a huge hole in the ground, into which he vanished and was never seen again!

Jack and his mother lived happily ever after, together with the golden harp and the little brown hen, and of course, their cow named Buttercup.

THE PRINCESS AND THE PEA

Once upon a time, there was a young Prince who decided to get married. "You must marry a real, genuine Princess," insisted his mother the Queen. "She must be beautiful, clever, charming and kind. Nothing less will do!" And with that, she ordered the Prince's horse to be saddled and told him to ride off and start looking at once.

As there were no Princesses in his own kingdom, the Prince had to travel to every country in the world to look for one.

He met lots of them on his journey, but not one was perfect. Some were too tall and some were much too small, others too fat and some too thin. Some were very old and some were just babies.

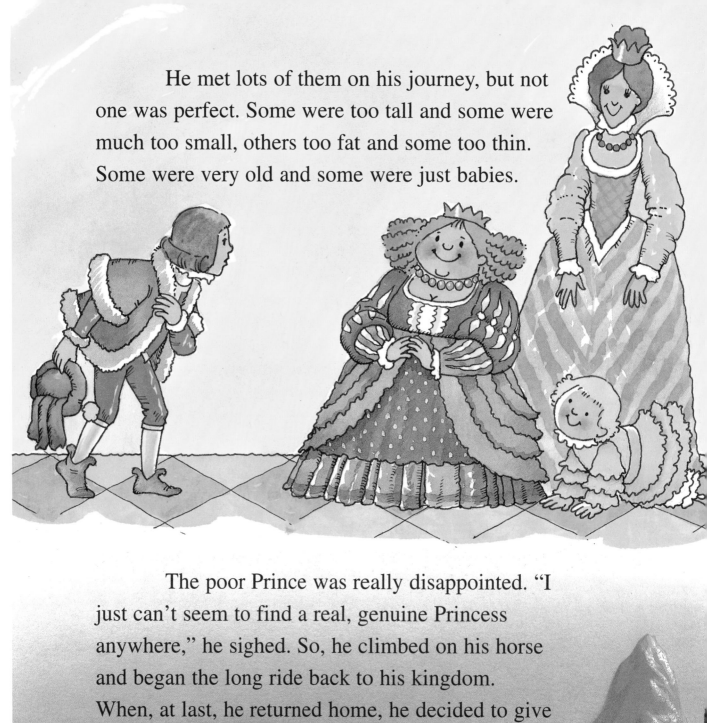

The poor Prince was really disappointed. "I just can't seem to find a real, genuine Princess anywhere," he sighed. So, he climbed on his horse and began the long ride back to his kingdom. When, at last, he returned home, he decided to give up the idea all together.

One dark night there
was the most terrible storm. The
wind howled and the rain fell by
the bucketful. Great flashes of
lightning lit up the sky, and
thunder shook the palace walls.

In spite of all this noise,
the King heard the tiniest knock
on the palace door.

"Now, who can be calling on a night like
this?" snorted the Queen, for she was warm and
comfortable and did not want to be disturbed.
However, the kindly old King got up from his chair
and went to open the door himself.

There standing in the doorway, was a young
girl. Her clothes were soaking and her shoes were
spattered with mud. Rainwater ran down her face and
her long golden hair was all wet and bedraggled. What
a sight she looked!

"I am a Princess. Please may I come in?" she
whispered.

"Princess or not," said the King. "Come in by
the fire and get warm," and he led her by the hand into
the great hall of his palace.

When the Prince saw her standing in the
firelight, he fell in love with her and wanted to marry
her at once.

The Queen took one look at the girl dripping water on her best carpet and frowned. "She can't be a real, genuine Princess and look such a mess," she muttered to herself. "I've never heard such a tale in all my life!"

With that, she marched off towards the palace kitchens. And there, from the store cupboard, she took one tiny dried pea. Then she crept quietly up the back stairs into the very best guest room.

"We'll soon see if she's a real, genuine Princess," and she placed the pea right in the centre of the Princess's bed.

Next, the Queen sent for all the maids in the palace, "Bring me twenty mattresses from your linen cupboard at once."

The maids looked surprised, but were soon scurrying up and down the corridors puffing and panting under the weight of all those mattresses.

Pile them up high on the bed!" yelled the Queen. "Now fetch me twenty of your softest feather quilts," the Queen ordered in her sternest voice. So the maids brought the feather quilts. By now everyone was quite out of breath.

"Now place the twenty feather quilts on top of the twenty mattresses," the Queen went on.

The pile of mattresses was so high that the maids could no longer reach them. So the Queen ordered her pageboys to bring long ladders. They pulled the twenty quilts up the ladders until, at last, the job was done and the Queen was satisfied.

While all this was going on the Princess had dried out from her soaking and was ready for bed.

She climbed up the ladder right to the top of the twenty mattresses and twenty feather quilts.

"Now we shall see if she is a real, genuine Princess," smiled the Queen.

Next morning, the storm had passed. The wind had died down and the storm clouds had gone from the sky. Bright sunshine streamed in through the palace windows, and it was a beautiful day.

The Princess, however, came in to breakfast looking very pale and tired.

"Did you sleep well?" the Queen asked her.

"No, indeed I did not," she replied with a yawn. "In fact, I couldn't sleep a wink." And the poor Princess rubbed her back. "I think I must have been lying on a rock, the bed felt so hard and uncomfortable."

The Prince looked at the King in dismay – but the Queen told them not to worry. How she laughed as she led the Princess back to her bedroom.

One by one the pageboys took away the feather quilts. Then one by one the maids took away the mattresses. And there, lying right in the middle of the bed, was one tiny dried PEA!

"Only a real, genuine Princess could feel a tiny dried pea through all those quilts and mattresses," laughed the Queen with delight.

When the Prince heard the story he asked the Princess to marry him. Not because she had proved she was a real, genuine Princess – but because he had fallen in love with her when he first saw her.

So, the Prince married the Princess and they were very happy together.

They kept the tiny dried pea on a velvet cushion inside a special glass case. This would keep it quite safe. In the years to come their children could take a look at it – and in many years, perhaps their grandchildren too!

HANSEL AND GRETEL

Once upon a time, there lived on the edge of a dark forest a poor woodcutter, his wife and two children. The little boy was called Hansel and the little girl's name was Gretel.

When the children were small, the woodcutter had lots of work and everyone had plenty to eat. But sad to say, their happiness did not last. The woodcutter's wife died, and the poor man chose another, who turned out to be cruel and selfish.

One day a great famine came to the land, leaving everyone short of food. The poor woodcutter was very worried as they had only one piece of bread left. His family would soon starve.

Hansel and Gretel's cruel stepmother made sure that she wouldn't starve. "Tomorrow morning, take the children to the thickest part of the forest, an leave them," she said. "Someone may come along and take pity on them and perhaps give them some food. For if they stay with us they will starve anyway."

She pleaded and argued so much that the woodcutter was forced to agree with her evil suggestion. Hansel and Gretel had not been able to sleep, because they were so hungry. And they heard every word their parents had said.

"Don't cry, Gretel," said the boy to his little sister, "for I have thought of a plan to find our way home again."

The moon was shining brightly as Hansel
climbed out of his bedroom window and jumped
down onto the path. He filled both his pockets with
small white pebbles, then crept quietly back to bed.

Early next morning, the poor woodcutter led
his children deeper and deeper into the forest.

Clever Hansel trailed behind, pretending to be
watching the birds. Every so often he let fall a shiny
white pebble from his pocket.

When it grew dark, the woodcutter built a
huge fire. His children were so tired that they fell
asleep in front of it. When they woke up, their father
had gone.

Little Gretel was very frightened, and began to cry. "Don't worry," Hansel told his sister. "Wait until the moon comes out."

Once the moon had risen, the children could see the pebbles shining brightly on the forest path. They followed them, and by morning they were home.

Their father was overjoyed to see his dear children again, but their cruel stepmother was very angry because her plan had failed.

It wasn't long before she began to argue and plead with the woodcutter once more. "There is not enough food left to feed us all," she screamed. "Get rid of your children, or we shall all die."

This time (to make sure the woodcutter made
no more mistakes), the stepmother went along to see
that Hansel and Gretel were left to die in the forest.

However, she did not notice Hansel throwing
down tiny crumbs of bread onto the forest path.

Once again, the woodcutter made the children
a roaring fire, and once again they both fell fast asleep.

When the children woke up and found
themselves alone, they began to search for the
breadcrumbs. But, alas, the birds had eaten them all
up. Poor Hansel and Gretel, they sat down and cried
themselves to sleep by the fire.

In the morning, when it grew light, the two set
off to find their way home. In fact, they were just walking
round in circles – deeper and deeper into the forest.

It was then that Hansel noticed a tiny white
bird sitting on a branch. The bird began to sing,
"Follow me, follow me." It flew in front of the
children until it reached a little house in a clearing.

It was the most unusual house you could
dream of. The walls were made of gingerbread and
the roof of cake and biscuits. The windows were sugar
and the doors were peppermint sticks. Hansel and
Gretel were so hungry that they began to eat bits and
pieces off the house.

Then the door opened
and an old woman hobbled out. At first
the children drew back in fear.
"Come inside, my dears," she
smiled, "and I will look after you."

The old woman cooked
them a lovely dinner, and showed
them two little beds covered with
soft pillows and blankets. That
night the children fell asleep
thinking they were safe and sound
at last.

Poor Hansel and Gretel. They had fallen right
into a trap. The old woman was really a witch whose
favourite food was children!

Very early next morning, the witch grabbed
the sleeping Hansel and locked him in a cage.

Next, she shook Gretel hard. "Wake up girl and cook your brother a huge breakfast. When he is fat enough I shall eat him."

Day after day, Gretel had to cook huge meals to fatten-up her brother.

Now, the witch was very short-sighted. Every morning she would make Hansel stick his finger out of the cage – just to see how much he had grown. But the boy was crafty. Instead of his finger, he would poke a chicken bone through the bars. "You're still too thin," she would scream, and make Gretel cook even more food.

Week after week went by, until the witch could wait no longer. "I shall eat him right away!" she cackled.

Without wasting a moment, the old witch
dragged Gretel into the kitchen. She made the terrified
girl stoke the fire until the oven was red hot. "Is the
oven ready for roasting?" called the witch with glee.

"I cannot tell," answered Gretel, pretending
not to understand.

This made the witch very angry. "Stupid
girl," she cried, as she pulled Gretel across the room.
"This is how it's done," and the witch bent over and
stuck her head in the oven.

Gretel gave her one great push, and the evil
witch fell inside and was burnt to a crisp.

Swiftly, Gretel freed her brother from that
awful cage, and the children danced for joy.

Before they left for home, they found a pile
of gold hidden in the witch's cottage.

Then, as if by magic, a new path opened up
through the forest. It led to a broad river where a great
white duck was waiting to take them across.

Very soon they saw their own dear house
through the trees. Their wicked stepmother had died,
and their father was a sad and sorry man.

Luckily, Hansel and Gretel soon forgot about
the wicked witch. They forgave their poor father and
all lived happily every after.

THE PIED PIPER OF HAMELIN

Long, long ago in Hamelin Town, Germany, something happened almost too strange to tell. Nevertheless, this story has been passed down through generations of parents to their children – until it has become a legend.

The town of Hamelin lay on the banks of the River Weser. It was a very pleasant place to live. The people of the town were prosperous and had more than enough to eat. Their pantries and larders were piled high with rich, tasty food, and their cellars were packed with the best wines. They wore the finest clothes of velvet trimmed with fur, and shoes of the softest leather.

But one night, all this came to an end!

As the people slept safe and warm in their beds, suddenly, without any warning, the whole town was overrun by rats. They swarmed over the high town walls by the thousands. They scurried down the dark streets pouring into houses through cellars and drains. Their rustling and squeaking quickly aroused the townsfolk. They jumped out of bed in horror, to find great black rats clambering up the stairs and running over their bedroom floors.

Soon, the whole town was awake, and lights began to appear in every window. It didn't take the people long to realise they had been completely invaded by a sea of rats. They tried in vain to drive

them out of their houses, chasing them out with sticks and pokers, in fact, anything they could lay their hands on. But it was no good!

To make matters worse, the plague of rats began to eat everything in sight. They gobbled all the food from the tables. They ran across the kitchen stoves and ate the stew and soup straight from the bubbling pans. There were rats in the flour sacks, rats in the milk churns, and every scrap of butter and cheese vanished in a trice. They even stole the loaves of hot bread baking in the ovens! It wasn't long before every scrap of food in the town had disappeared, eaten by the rats. The shops were all empty, even the taverns had no food or drink left.

Everyone began to feel hungry for the first time, and they were worried that they might soon starve. Something must be done! The people of Hamelin were desperate. Groups of them gathered on street corners muttering and complaining. Then they started to march through the town, joining together until they formed a great crowd outside the Town Hall, where everyone began to shout for the Mayor.

The crowd sounded so angry that the Mayor's knees knocked together with fright. He had been locked in his chamber with all the town councillors for days. Not one of them could think of a solution.

All at once the crowd grew quiet. A stranger appeared from nowhere, stepped up to the Town Hall, knocked on the Mayor's door and went inside!

He was the strangest figure – his queer long coat, from heel to head, was half of yellow and half of red. He himself was tall and thin, with sharp blue eyes, each like a pin.

The stranger spoke up, "If I rid your town of rats, will you give me a thousand gilders?"

The Mayor stared in astonishment, "I will give you not one thousand gilders, but fifty thousand!"

Around the stranger's neck hung a pipe. "People call me the Pied Piper," he said, and without another word he stepped into the street and started to play. He had only uttered three notes, when the rats began to appear. They poured out of the houses and into the streets in their thousands, following the music as if they were bewitched. Through the streets the Piper led the rats, out of the town gates, until he came to the banks of the River Weser.

There the Pied Piper stopped his playing, and as if with one accord, the rats jumped into the river and were drowned! A mighty cheer went up from all the townsfolk watching from the walls. How they cheered the Pied Piper as he went back to collect his reward from the Mayor.

As he reached the Town Hall the Mayor shouted from the steps, "Be off with you, Piper!" I owe you nothing for just playing one tune." Then the Mayor laughed in the Piper's face. "The rats are gone and can't come back, go blow your pipe 'til you burst!"

Once more the Piper stepped into the street. He put his pipe to his lips again and began to blow. The notes he played were so sweet that all the crowds in the street stopped, spellbound by the music.

Then, there came such a rustling and a bustling. Small feet were pattering, wooden shoes clattering, little hands clapping and little tongues chattering. Out came the children running. All the little boys and girls with rosy cheeks and flaxen curls were tripping and skipping, running merrily after that wonderful music with shouts and laughter.

The Mayor, the council and the parents stood, as if they were changed into blocks of wood, unable to move a step or cry out as the children merrily skipped by. The Piper led them through the gate of the town. On and on they danced, over fields, down lanes, until they were far into the countryside. How the townsfolk cried and called after their children, but they didn't seem to hear.

Suddenly, the Piper turned his steps towards the mountains, and the townspeople's cries turned to joy. "He can't cross that mountain top," the Mayor sighed with relief. "He must let his piping drop, and then our children will stop."

As the children reached the mountain side, a great door opened wide. The Piper went in and the children followed. And when they were all safe inside – the door in the mountain shut fast.

All except one little boy, as he was lame, he couldn't dance the whole of the way. Unable to keep up with the others, he had been left behind.

The Mayor of Hamelin searched far and wide for the Pied Piper, offering all the gold and silver in the town, if only the Piper could bring the children back. But Piper and children were gone forever.

The legend says they went to a better land where people always keep their promises – especially to Pipers!